Ruby Long Dog Goes on Holiday

by Lindsey Kennedy

illustrated by Alicia Howard

This Ruby Long Dog Tale

is dedicated to

Johnny, Charlie, and Emily

Ruby Long Dog is a long red dog called a Dachshund.

Ruby Long Dog noticed that her family had taken the suitcases down from the loft. There was a big pile of things in the middle of the room. Ruby Long Dog had a good sniff!

Ruby Long Dog asked Aunty Daisy what could possibly be happening. Aunty Daisy reassured Ruby Long Dog. She told her that they were going to the seaside, and it was going to be lots of fun.

The next day they all set off. The car was full. There was barely room for Ruby Long Dog and Aunty Daisy in the boot!

When they arrived at the holiday cottage it looked beautiful, and Ruby Long Dog could see the sea in the distance.

Before long another family arrived at the cottage. They had a dog called Harry. Harry was a springy Springer Spaniel!

🐾 There are various breeds of spaniels –

Springer Spaniel

Cocker Spaniel

King Charles Spaniel

Water Spaniel

Soon they all set off to explore the seaside.
They walked along the promenade past a row of very colourful beach huts.

The families decided it was time for a cup of
tea at Susie's beach café.

Ruby Long Dog and Aunty Daisy, and Harry were being good, but a large seagull was being very naughty. The big bird was trying to take a cake from one of the tables.

Some cafés, pubs, hotels and restaurants are dog friendly. Look out for the Dog Friendly signs and welcoming water bowls.

Dogs Welcome

The next day the families spent the day on the beach. Ruby Long Dog, Aunty Daisy and Harry all had a play in the sea.

The dogs were allowed off their leads to run along the footpath.

🐾 You must **always** remember to pick up your dog's poo and put it in the correct rubbish bin.

DOG POO ONLY

Ruby Long Dog and Aunty Daisy were excited because it was the day for the 'Seaside Sausage Dog Walk'!

🐾 Many seaside towns and other cities have a dog walk every year, where Dachshund dog owners gather and walk their dogs altogether.

Ruby Long Dog and Aunty Daisy had never seen so many dogs like them. There were black and tan ones, red ones like Ruby Long Dog Dog, and spotty ones. Some with short hair, some with long hair and some with crazy hair!

The families and dogs all went down to the harbour.
There were lots of those naughty seagulls looking for
tasty treats.

They saw some children crabbing on the jetty. Ruby Long Dog did not like the idea of her nose getting pinched by the crab's claws.

After lunch they boarded the rowing boat ferry that took them across the river estuary.

🐾 Dogs can wear life jackets on board a boat.

On their way back to the cottage Ruby Long Dog, Auntie Daisy, and Harry were surprised to see dray horses plodding down the road, pulling a heavy load.

The families wanted to buy some postcards and went into town to look around the shops.

They saw their friends Doug and Fred, the Standard Poodles, with their friend, Ron, another Dachshund. Standard Poodles are large elegant dogs with curly hair.

🐾 There are 5 different types of poodles, all different sizes – Standard, Miniature, Toy, Klein, and Teacup.

It was so exciting on the pier, with interesting sounds and smells.

Ruby Long Dog was very nervous as she walked along the pier. She didn't like the gaps in the planks of wood. You could see the sea below through the gaps.

🐾 Sometimes dogs are nervous on piers or bridges where there are gaps in the wooden planks. Little dogs, like miniature Dachshunds, should be carried.

The end of the holiday came all too soon for the dogs. Ruby Long Dog slept all the way home. She dreamt about having so much fun at the seaside. She dreamt about the colourful beach huts, the sausage dog walk, playing on the beach, the rowing boat trip ...

... but mostly about those noisy, naughty seagulls!

About the Dogs

All the dogs in these tales were or are real dogs that live with their families in the beautiful Buckinghamshire countryside.

Ruby is a red Smooth Haired Miniature Dachshund. She is a cheeky little dog with a large character and inspired Lindsey's Long Dog tales. Children are always admiring her.

Daisy was a Wire Haired Miniature Dachshund. She lived to the great age of 16. She loved Ruby and looked after her as if she was her own puppy!

Harry is a Harry is a 9 year old Springer Spaniel. He's very very energetic and needs lots of exercise. He loves swimming, chasing balls, carrying round cuddly toys and eating! His favourite place is definitely the seaside!

Doug and Fred are Standard Poodles. They adore their human family and the other pets who live with them — Ron the Dachshund and Daisy the Cockapoo. Fred likes stretching out on the rug in front of the fire. Doug is very lively, and turns everything into a game.

Ron is a black and tan Smooth Haired Miniature Dachshund. He loves trying to run as fast as Doug and Fred, but never catches up with them.

Ruby and Daisy at the seaside

Harry

Doug and Fred

Ron

About the Authors

Lindsey Kennedy grew up in London, but has lived in the beautiful Buckinghamshire countryside for 40 years. She has taught in Early Years and Key Stage1 Education. She has four sons and five little grandchildren. Lindsey has always had a yearning to write stories for children and this is her first published series. Daisy was Lindsey's first dachshund, Ruby her second. Lindsey has a passion for animals and countryside living, and enjoys teaching horse-riding to the disabled.

Alicia Howard lives and works as a designer and illustrator in a little village in Buckinghamshire, having moved there from London with her husband and children over 25 years ago. Brought up and educated in the North of England, she moved South to study Graphic Design. She worked in the publishing industry for many years, including the educational sector, designing books for primary school children. She enjoys family life, especially making art and crafts with her grandchildren, and reading them bedtime stories.

Other Ruby Long Dog Tales

Look out for more stories about Ruby Long Dog and her friends ~

Ruby Long Dog

Ruby Long Dog Visits the Vet

Ruby Long Dog's First Christmas

First published in Great Britain in 2022
by Long Dog Books

ISBN 978-1-3999-1845-9

Printed by CLOC Ltd
Unit 10 Milmead Industrial Estate, Mill Mead Road,
Tottenham, London N17 9QU